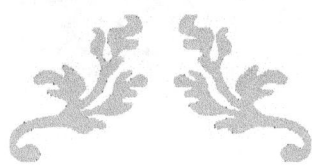

DANGEROUS DANA

Dana Can't Be Stopped

PRESENT

**Dangerous
Dana**

Is a Bad Girl

By: *Jonnie Dauphine*

Reach The Press Publishing
14051Belle Chasse Blvd Unit 213
Laurel, Maryland 20707

Printed in the United States of America

Introduction

This book is a thrilling short story about a young lady who was abused in a foster home, and she had multiple personality disorder, is characterized by a person's identity fragmenting into two or more distinct personality states. Her condition was from her being a victim of severe abuse. One personality was a timid young lady, and the other one was dangerous, fearless you did not want to mess with her. This story about Dana is a captivating story about love and revenge.

Where Dana takes up for her Alissa,
who was bashful and fearful, not willing
to fight. When Alissa found out some
unsuspecting news. That was
devastating to her and Dana told her not
to worry about it she would handle it.
Alissa was not sure how Dana was
going to take care of the situation but
step back out of the way when she and
Dana had a clear understanding of what
was going on in her house. The
situation got ugly after that Dana was
distraught that Alissa was being played
for a fool. She felt like Alissa was her
sister after all that they had been
through in the foster home.

Dana thought that she had to take care of Alissa and look out for her. So, she took the matter into her own hands. Dana with into a rage that no one could stop her, and the outcome was deadly.

Dangerous Dana

Alissa and Paul were enjoying brunch on a beautiful sunny spring day after attending church. Paul sat across from Alissa in tan slacks, a powder blue blazer with a white shirt, and brown Christian Louboutin leather loafers. He was flawlessly delivering color and style to an already beautiful day.

Paul's signature bald head glistened in the sun, and his hazel completion looked flawless against his choice of attire.

Paul was one of Alissa's best friends, she never judged him for being gay, and he never judged her colorful past. Alissa loved Paul as if he were her flesh and blood and she always admired how outspoken and fashionable he was.

She still found herself staring at his designer wear and wondered how he could afford them on a fast food manager budget, but that was none of her business.

Alissa olive complexion glistens in the sun, and her green eyes were mesmerizing.

Her slant to her eyes always gave reasons for people to ask if she

was mixed race, which she was half

Black and Laotians.

She could thank her daddy for

the slants, olive complexion, and high

cheekbones, but that ass, small waist,

and them Double D's came straight

from the motherlands.

The sun was shining, and there

was a lovely breeze dancing

throughout the picturesque May Day

in Michigan. They decided to take in the sights of the day and sit on the patio of a local bistro and enjoy their spread of pastries, fruits, and mimosa.

The two friends were engaging in casual conversation when Alissa switch the direction of the conversation.

"I really love Gavin, and I can't wait to be his wife someday. We're going to make beautiful babies I just

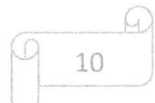

know it." Said Alissa as she twirled her curly brown hair between her fingers.

"Are you sure he is ready for such a huge step?" said Paul between sips of his drink.

"I think so it been almost 5 years, I'm not going to wait around forever."

"If I was you, I would wait around for Mr. Right, because that nigga clearly Mr. Wrong.

I'm sorry to take you off your high horse Sis, but Gavin ain't shit, and the sooner you notice, the better off you will be."

"I know he isn't perfect, but we love each other, and that's all that matters. When two...."

"You dumber than three bricks laying in the sun! He's an ain't shit nigga, he don't want marriage he wants a place to stay. I don't think that nigga want the same things you want."

Alissa lowered her head and began to stare down at her plate of food as tears started to build. She did not know how to address this man that she thought was her friend. The more her mind began to race and fill with

emotions the easier it was for Alissa

friend to show up.

"Alissa don't take this shit

personally, I'm just telling you the

truth about your adult foster child,"

Paul said.

Alissa didn't flinch, she did not

speak, she just continued to stare

aimlessly at the uneaten food on her

plate as she held a tight grip of the

fork in her right hand.

"Alissa! Alissa! Alissa!" Paul

called out to her.

Alissa slowly picked her head

up and locked her sight on Paul. She

stood up from the table with the fork

still in her hand and lean over to Paul.

In a very calm voice, she told Paul,

"Don't you ever in your life fix your cock sucking lips to spill some shit around me like that. If you ever decide you gonna let your mouth run like that I guarantee you that bitch will be wired tight."

Alissa straightens out her sundress over her thick curvy physique, dropped the fork, and put her sunshades over her eyes and started walking away. While walking away, a thought crossed her mind, and she turned around. She cocked back and threw a left hook that landed right in the center of Paul's face. His face fell onto the table sending drinks and food flying everywhere. She reached into his pocket and grabbed his wallet, turned around and walked away.

"Now who's the dumb brick laying in the sun bitch," Alissa said as her booty jiggled while she walked away from a totally knocked out Paul.

"Babe are you home," Alissa called for Gavin as she entered their apartment. There was no answer, but she could hear movement throughout the house coming from the direction of her bedroom. Alissa closed the door softly and began to move in the direction of the noise. The house was dark and smelled of a fruity fragrance with slow music playing low in the back grown.

"I know damn well this nigga better not have one of these dusty, dirty feet thirsty ass thots in my house," Alissa said as anger began to grow inside her. She headed for the kitchen and grabbed the biggest knife she could find because if the situation was what she thought no one was leaving alive. Gavin had never once given her any reason to believe that he may be cheating, but baby Alissa was ready for war. Rage began to take over her body as she made quick and steady movements toward the sound of the music and opened her bedroom door.

The room was dark, but as soon as her eyes focus, she could not believe her sight.

The knife fell to the floor as Alissa screamed Gavin's name on top of him was her best friend, Paul. Paul was serving male beefcake to her beloved boyfriend who was too busy enjoying himself to notice Alissa walk in, but Paul wasn't. Paul started putting on a show for his dear old friend and add a slick smile to fuel an already burning Alissa. Seconds before Alissa vision clearly saw the devastating scene, Paul heard the door open and did not even make any effort to stop, in fact, he turned up with Gavin to occupy him long enough for Alissa to walk through her bedroom and see the queen she loves so much.

Alissa was stuck in a state of confusion; she physically could not move. Gavin on the other was just getting to know his new reality, he scrambled to cover himself up as he started on his story to make his love believe this was not real. Maybe he would tell her Paul was helping fix the television. One stuck, one lying, and one laughing. Paul laughed and laughed at them as Alissa and Gavin's world came crashing down around them.

Little did Alissa know that she was the butt of an ugly revenge plot by her so call best friend.

Alissa and Gavin had drain Paul's

bank accounts and tried to cover it up,

but Paul knew.

Paul had been giving Gavin the long

and strong for months. Actually,

Gavin was one of Paul's clients and

was one of the reasons why Paul

could afford to be dripped in designer

wear. It was time to let Alissa know

what Gavin was really into so, he

texted Alissa from Gavin's phone and

told her there was something she needed to see to come home quick. Alissa came home to this bullshit.

Paul was doing this just for the thrill, but while he was laughing Alissa had intentions to kill. See what Paul or Gavin didn't know was Alissa wasn't alone. Paul's laughter had just triggered her partner in crime to the point of no return, and there was no stopping Dana.

In rushed Dana, as she picked

up the knife that Alissa just dropped

on the floor. She started swinging the

knife left to right as she did her wet

work on the unexpected Paul who was

still laughing as he sat on the bed.

Dana slice Paul from ear to his mouth

as viciousness began to build inside of

her. The next swing cut his hands

open as he tried to stop Dana from

cutting him again, but he just pissed

her off even more. Dana started to

stab Paul in his chest and with one

raise of her murder weapon Paul's

body fell to the floor, lifeless. Dana

picked up her head after she gave

Paul's body a look of admiration, she

always took pleasure in taking out the

trash. She could see in her far right

the sheets slide off the bed and notice

Gavin body hiding under the sheet her

new target was in range, and Dana was ready.

Gavin didn't hear anything and thought maybe Alissa had taken control of the situation, so he poked his head out from under the sheet. All Gavin saw was a pair of green eyes looking at him. Gavin took no time to escape and ran from around the bed with the brown queen size sheet wrapped around him as he darted out of the bedroom door pass Alissa who was still stuck on stupid.

Dana stood there looking at Gavin like a fool as he entered the long dark hallway. He was naked, running, and screaming. The scene was funny to Dana, but it also added some excitement to it. Dana walked out of the bedroom into the hallway and entered the family room where she met up with a very nervous Gavin

who was still trying to figure out how to unlock the door.

A smile grew on Dana's face because she was going to make Gavin pay for his cheating ways.

Dana loved Alissa like a sister because they grow up in the same foster home and sometimes shared the same abuse. Alissa took her abuse and became shy and timid, but Dana was downright dangerous. Dana felt like

Alissa was her sister and that Alissa was a part of her, she even felt at times they were the same person. It wasn't a good feeling to see her sister in a situation like this so these men would have to pay the ultimate price for her pain.

Dana strolled slowly towards Gavin as he held the doorknob in the dim lit family room. Gavin's nerves were on edge as he looked back at

Dana walking toward him while he was still trying to escape.

Within inches of him, Dana picked up the knife and pointed it at him and said "You thought you was just going to get away I know your loose lips told that trick Paul we robbed him." Now, look what that bitch ass nigga fucked up and made me do. Fuck I always gotta clean up the fucking mess!"

"I didn't say anything I swear......I love you" said Gavin while he looked at this woman confused about what was coming next.

She gave him a slight grin and whisper you don't know what love is and she went to work on his ass. Dana delivered a kick to Gavin's back that severed his spine causing him to be paralyzed from the waist down. Gavin's grip from the doorknob did not loosen as his body hit the carpet floor. Dana approached him still holding the knife, she stood over him and watch as he opened up the flood gates and cried a river. Dana begins slicing him up while she talked to him.

"You're a disloyal motherfucker."

(slice)

"I knew you was no good for my girl from the first time I saw you." (slice, slice)

"You thought you was going to live after what you did to us, how you steal from a nigga and fuck him." (slice straight to the face)

"How you die, and your last drink was that nigga Paul seeds? Your dick in the booty ass closet freak." (slice on top the hand still holding the

doorknob)

Gavin let out a horrible scream

followed by a couple mumbles which

made Dana mad, so she began to

punch and kick Gavin until there was

nothing but dead silence surrounding

her. Dana fell to the floor, in the fetal

position, next to Gavin's lifeless

body.

The light-colored carpet, walls,

Gavin, and her were covered in

Gavin's blood as Dana rested her

head on her knees when she heard

Alissa's tiny voice say, "Is it all over."

Dana respond yes while she stood up

from the blood-soaked floor.

Alissa looked around the room at the

blood everywhere. She was confused

and could not understand what

happened.

"I cannot believe you did all of this,"
Alissa said to Dana.

"What else was I going to do you just
can't keep letting these niggas play
you no matter if you fucking them are
not." Dana said.

Alissa said, "Well I don't know."

Dana said "Well you know now"

Alissa said, "This is bad."

"Bitch bye this ain't bad them niggas was bad they mama should have swallowed and save us all some heartache," Dana said

Gavin's dead body laid in the front of the door as life was slipping from him. The last thing he saw before he met death was the woman, he loves standing there in the middle of the family room ALONE. As death gripped Gavin's body his sight did not deceive him, only one person was standing in the room.

Since childhood, Alissa had been abused both physically and mentally. Her mother died giving birth, and the stress of being a single father took a toll on her dad, so he turned to drugs. After being found in her dad's house at the age of five alone, she was put into the system where she bounced around from foster homes to group homes. While she was in the midst of it all a part of her wanted revenge on the people that caused her pain. The fragment of Alissa that wish to attack consumed her so much that it became a personality of its own who like to be called Dana. Alissa had perfect control of Dana but when her emotions became too much for her to handle Dana would gladly take over.

Dana was the reason this all
went down. Alissa and Paul were
having a conversation about marriage
that Paul did not agree about which
made Paul laugh at Alissa silly idea of
happy ever after. That bought out
Dana because Alissa was not happy.
Dana knocked Paul out with one
punch to his face. She dug into Paul's
pocket and stole his debit card and
cash. Dana left Paul leaking in the

middle of a crowded restaurant.

Before going home, she drained

Paul's accounts. She flashed all the

money she had just taken from Paul to

Gavin who was waiting back at home.

Gavin looked into his beloved

girlfriend's eyes and could tell

something wasn't right, but he was

more interested in the money.

Dana and Gavin splurged the

money on any and everything and

went home and had mind-blowing

sex. The best sex Gavin had ever had

with his girlfriend. The next morning

Alissa woke up with a severe

headache and a sore body. She was

aware of what happened when Dana

took over but the older she got, the

less she could control her. Alissa got

dress and went to work. She just

didn't know she would have to be the

one to pay for Dana's mistakes when she got back home.

Still standing in the middle of the living room the ladies continued their conversation

"So, what are we gonna do now?" said Alissa.

"Don't worry about this. I got you Ma like I always do. Just stay in your corner while I make these money moves." said Dana.

Alissa was uneasy, but she agreed to whatever Dana had planned because after all, they did share the same body. Dana took a long shower, put on some jeans and a T-shirt, and pulled her hair back into a ponytail. She maneuvered around the apartment as if there were not two bodies in the building tracking blood through the house giving new meaning to bloody

shoes. An hour later an unbothered

Dana was leaving the apartment with

two suitcases, one stuffed with Paul

and one stuffed with Gavin while the

apartment burned in the background.

"Why your dumb ass ditch the car and

got us walking on the side of this hot

ass highway with a fucking backpack on your back like a fucking lost school girl?" said Alissa.

"Just be cool love I got us besides we had to get rid of the luggage we was rolling with," said Dana reminding Alissa of the two dead niggas they were traveling with.

Dana left Alissa's car parked at a truck stop in Missouri and hitched a ride with a truck driver down to Lafayette,

Louisiana. Dana was dropped on the side of the highway after Dana gave the truck driver a new smile by slicing his face from ear to ear for trying to get in her cookie jar while she was asleep. She removed the blade out of her bra and swung at him giving him a new look that made him look like the Joker's twin.

"Dana, what if we get caught?" said Alissa.

"How the fuck we gonna get caught in a country ass little town like this?" said Dana swishing her full hips as she walked down the highway.

It was the middle of February, and it was seventy-five degrees out Dana was not accustomed to these temperatures because she was from Michigan. The city was covered in trees with homes and businesses scattered throughout the city. As Dana

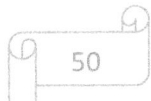

walked down the busy highway, she

caught the attention of a guy driving a

hunter green 2017 Dodge Challenger.

He pulled off the road right on the

side of Dana.

"Damn you must be tired dragging

that slug shorty you need a ride

somewhere?" the guy driving the

challenger said.

"What the hell are you talking about?"

said Dana turning around to stare in

the eyes of the most handsome hazel

eye man she had ever seen.

"I'm talking about that ass you

dragging back there. You lost are

something because damn sure never

seen you around here? I know your

man ain't letting your fine ass walk

around this city by yourself." the man

said in a very thick southern accent.

"Man look my ride dipped on me, and

I'm not from here so basically, I'm

stuck. I usually don't fuck with people

I don't know, but you a whole snack

so I'll take you up on that offer. What

I'm supposed to call you?" Dana said

while he propped up her double size

breast on her arms.

"Call me yours, are call me Body like

everyone else does."

"That's what ya momma named

you?"

"No, she named me Marlon, but my people call me Body. Get in Ma we going to get you set up at my spot in my guest room."

The young man called Body was admiring Dana's beauty. He took her in from head to toe. He noticed that she had very loose curly brown hair with slants to her green eyes and high cheekbones. She was bright like the sun with curves that would make any man are woman turn and look twice.

With her full breast tiny waist and her

huge ass, he just could not believe she

was single. Dana got into the car and

sat down Body couldn't stop himself

from thinking he wanted to be that

seat.

Dana looked at Body to take him all

in, he was at least six feet tall with

short jet-black coiled hair.

The top part of his hair was about two inches long while the sides where neatly trim and faded. It was evident to Dana that he worked out because as he held the stirring wheel with his right hand, his muscles bulged out of his shirt. He was just Dana's type caramel, pretty, with perfect teeth.

The two drove down Highway 90 in the direction of the city of Broussard, the words of *Middle Child* by J. Cole played softly from the speakers of the cars sounds systems.

"Look I live in a three-bedroom house you can stay in the guest room and don't worry Lil baby it has its own restroom." Body said.

"You look young ass fuck; how do you afford all this shit?" said Dana.

"What you wanna know all that shit for? You trynna let me put you on?"

"Depends on what you doing because I'm not selling no pussy and I'm damn sure ain't popping my pussy."

"I'm like FedEx I pick up and deliver, but shit I only do that shit once a year for the rest of the year I chase the bag through my many businesses."

"Is one of the businesses selling pussy because you pretty enough to trick a bitch into selling anything?"

"I thought you didn't notice how sexy I was, but no I don't sell pussy."

"What the fuck you deliver that you only pick up and deliver once a year?"

"Right now, it's Mardi Gras, and during parades, the police are more worried about the safety and security of the people enjoying the festivities more than people breaking the law. A couple of times throughout the parade schedule I pick up packages from

people that are on floats in the
parade."

"Wait slow down what the fuck is
Marda Grey and what the fuck is a
parade?"

"The easiest way to explain MARDI
GRAS is it's a big party right before
people make personal sacrifices
during the Lent season."

"Ok so it's one big sin before the blessing," said Dana while letting out a chuckle.

"Something like that, you ready to chase that bag are what?" The young man called Body said while swinging his car onto a road filled with brick homes and manicured lawns.

Body pulled up to a brick house, while he was pulling up a white garage door opened, and he pulled into the garage. The two walked into the house and Dana was immediately taken back by the décor of the home. There were hardwood floors similar to the color of coffee beans running throughout the house. The kitchen had white granite countertops that sat on top of soft grey cabinets. All his appliance was stainless steel, he even had a fully stock bar that broke up the space between the living area and the dining area. Beautiful artwork hung from the walls acting as the perfect accessories to his white oversized furniture.

"Nigga, I know fucking well a bitch gotta stay here with you all this shit is too matchy-matchy for just a man to stay here," said Dana.

Body just laughed. "So, a nigga can't have good taste and shit? Na, my mama, and sister helped me put this shit together". Body said.

"They did a damn good job!"

"Shit don't let my sister hear you say that. Let me show you where I'm putting you."

Body walked Dana down a dim lit hallway to the last door to the right of the hall. Dana walked into the room and was pleased by the décor of that room as well. The walls were painted a soft grey color, the bedding was all white with accent pillows of grey and rose gold. There was a huge rose gold mirror that hung from the walls and silver white and light pink trinkets all along the dresser top. The grey and silver upholstered headboard had little gems on the seams and the matching nightstands where mirror top. Dana tossed her backpack to the floor and jumped into the bed; her body began to sink into the bedding and mattress.

"I don't know why you being so nice, but I really appreciate it." Said, Dana

"Say, Less. Put my line in your phone in case you need something because I might not be here when you wake. 3372813308" Said Body while turned around and walked off into the hallway.

Dana happily obliged and took her

phone out her pocket and typed in the

numbers. After she was done, she sat

the phone on the nightstand next to

the bed. She dug into her bra and

pulled out her black 45 Glock and

placed it into the drawer of the

nightstand. Dana was exhausted and

proceeded to remove clothing out of

her backpack and went into the

bathroom to take a long overdue hot

shower. After she got out of the

restroom, she pulled back the white

comforter and climbed into bed. It

was not long before the memory foam

mattress, and 1800 thread count

sheets had her in dreamland.

Alissa laid on the sofa in a dark living

room as unfamiliar hands ran up her

legs toward her womanhood. Alissa

had been through this before at other

foster homes, but she thought that the Davis family was different and could give her something that the other families could not, safety and security. Harold Davis worked weeks on end on an offshore rig, and his wife Gwinn was a cafeteria worker at a local elementary school. The two of them never had kids, and Gwinn told the social worker she wanted an older girl to help mold her and help her see that having a support system is better than being alone.

When Alissa was first moved in Mr. Davis was not home, and Mrs. Davis treated her with so much love and respect that Alissa couldn't help but to feel safe. This was Harold's first night back home in over a month, and he thought it would be a good idea to get to know the new addition to his family over movies and popcorn.

Alissa was only fifteen and was excited to actually meet and hang out with Mr. Davis.

Alissa fell asleep laying on the big black sectional sofa while the second movie was playing. She was awakened by warm hands running up her legs. She figured if she stayed still long enough, he would think that she was sleeping and leave her alone. She was wrong. His hands continued to roam her young adolescent body until

he found her center. He rubbed her

while she felt the warmth of his lips

meet the back of her neck. The faint

smell of beer and chewing tobacco

almost made her gag, but she stayed

perfectly still. She could hear

footsteps coming her way and hoped

and prayed that it was Gwinn and that

this nightmare would end soon.

Gwinn walked into the living room and stood over Harold and Alissa.

"Harold, what the fuck do you think you're doing?" Gwinn said while holding her robe close with one hand and smacking Harold behind the head with the other.

"You suppose to wait for me you selfish son of a bitch!" Gwinn said while delivering a blow to the back of Alissa's head.

"Wake up Bitch! It's time for us to give you the proper introduction into the Davis family!"

Harold's touch went from gentle to rough really quick as he grabbed Alissa by her waist and turned her around to face him and his monster of a wife. Gwinn removed her hand from her robe revealing her pale white skin, saggy titties, and furball pussy. Harold black ass was on his knees tugging on Alissa's shorts, all you really could see from that midnight nigga was his eyes.

"Stop acting like your ass innocent because as big as them titties and ass is, I know ya hoe has been ran through." Gwinn said as she grabbed Alissa's throat.

"Don't take it easy on this Lil bitch I want you to fuck the shit out of her while I show her what a real woman tastes like. Oh, and don't worry pretty

bitch no one will hear you scream and

if you move too much, I will kill your

young ass. Ain't nobody checking for

no missing foster child." Said Gwinn

as she loosens the grip around

Alissa's neck and positions herself on

top of Alissa's face laying all her

womanhood onto Alissa's face.

In less than five minutes Alissa had

blacked out while the couple violated

her, at that exact moment Dana was born.

Alissa woke up in a cold sweat gasping for air. She sat up in the bed and glanced around the dark room, she was shaking. She spent the rest of the night in the fetal position crying with the darkness of the room surrounding her.

The next morning Alissa's eyes were puffy from all the tears she shed, but

Alissa was forced back into her

corner, and a pissed off Dana emerged

with murder on her mind. Dana

picked up her phone that laid

peacefully on top of the mirrored

nightstand. The first person she called

was Body.

"Hey nigga, I'll help you with your

pickups and deliveries, but I need you

to help me to find some old friends of

mind." Dana said while she sat at the

edge of the bed pulling the nightstand drawer open and rubbing her Glock.

"I need a reunion of families to happen. I won't rest until my people bond." Dana spoke into the phone.

"Say less, shot me the names and I'll get my nigga Bun on that shit ASAP. We gon break bread on that other business later." Body said.

"Bet," Dana said as she laid back on the queen-sized bed, the white linens engulfed her body as she began to work on her master plan.

Dana and Body sat at the cherry oak dining table as Body broke down the plan on how Dana would pick up her package off of the floats along the parade route.

"Look I'm sending you to a little town call St. Martinville the parade they are

having is called the New Comers

Parade. The city will be

overcrowded with people from all

over enjoying this almost three-hour

parade. You don't have to worry

about the laws because they ain't got

enough mother fuckers to cover the

parade route let along worry about

niggas breaking the law. I'm giving

you this shirt to wear so my people

can know who they looking for.

You're picking up five bags." Body,

said while handing her a black shirt

that had some bleach stands and holes

on it, but the front read Slapface

Records in bold white letters with

some kind of goofy face on it.

"Is this a knockoff version of Kayne

clothing and what the fuck is a

Slapface," Dana said while holding

the shirt up with both hands.

"Don't worry about all that just wear the shirt and be in the city no later than 10 am the parade starts at 3pm. Oh, and another thing observes the people around you and try to fit into your surroundings. I don't want none of them jackers to be on to you."

"Bet," Dana said while getting up and proceeding to her room to get ready for her new adventure.

The traffic getting into the city of St. Martinville was ridiculous. Cars were lined up for miles, people were walking along the highway, music blasting, and the smell of smoked meat was heavy in the air. Everywhere Dana looked was a sign for no parking or a blocked off yard. She finally gave in and paid a man 10 dollars to park in his yard. According to the man she was lucky because his location was not too far from a prime location along the parade route.

Dana walked in the direction of loud music and huge crowds of people. Everyone was dress nice, laughing, rolling their ice chest, and carrying large bottles of liquor. Dana couldn't help but think that this would be more fun than she expected. When she reached the roadway, that was flooded with people, she was on a block with a restaurant that was directly across the street from a dollar store. People were eating food, dancing, selling stuff, talking, and just having a grand time. She looked at her watch, and it was only 1 pm, the city was crowded for as far as her eyes could see in either direction.

Dana didn't know what to do are where to go as it seems that everyone around her was a part of a group. She looked more confused than she

thought because she felt that all eyes

were on her. An older lady walked up

to her and gently tugged on her left

arm. Dana turned swiftly with her

hand already in her shirt.

"Hey, my baby you look lost are you

looking for someone." said the old

woman.

Dana looked down at the older lady

who was so petite. Dana was five feet

seven inches, so the lady was maybe a good four feet tall.

"Oh, this is my first time to one of these things I'm from Michigan; we don't do these types of things," Dana said while slowly removing her hand from her shirt.

"Well, then we gotta make sure you have a good time sugar, so you can come back every year." The older lady said.

"That's not necessary."

"Nonsense sha, come over here and get you some food honey. I know how you young folks can be, so I'll get my grandbaby to fix you a drink."

Before Dana knew it, she was surrounded by a crowd of people, with a plate of food and desserts in one hand, and a mixed drink and soft drink in the other. After she was done devouring the massive plate of ribs,

sausage, beans, macaroni and cheese,

she washed it down with cake and

something the locals called praline.

She had to admit it was the best food

she had in her life. When she was

finished, the older lady began to

introduce her to members of her crew.

She met grandbabies, nieces,

nephews, sons, daughters, sisters, and

brothers. Each person she met greeted

her with a warm embrace and a kiss

on the cheek. She had never felt so

welcomed and loved in her life.

By the time she could see pickup

trucks pulling colorful trailers she felt

so comfortable that she was no longer

nervous about receiving her packages.

She could see that the people on the

floats were throwing stuff animals,

necklaces, balls, and candy off the

trailers. She notices that the people in

the front of the crowds with their

hands up making noise seemed to get

the best stuff. As the first float

approached where she was standing,

she maneuvered through the crowd to

get in the front.

The first float came and went she was

embraced by members of the old

lady's family as they began to cover

her neck and shoulders with multi-

colored beads. The second float

slowly approached, and she began to

dance to the tune of Juvenile's *Back That Azz Up*. Her inner THOT was coming out as the float rolled in front of them. Someone dressed in a funny costume covered in feathers and different colors handed her a bag of beads. She threw her hands up to receive the pack while still twerking. One package down four to go.

The end of the parade was near, and Dana had collected all her packages along with a couple of stuff animals and other toys. She was just about to leave the parade route with a grocery bag filled with her collectibles when she felt a tap on her back. Dana did not hesitate to reach into her shirt for her Glock as she turned around and saw a man standing there rocking the same ugly face shirt.

"Be cool Lil baby!" The nigga said while putting his hands up. He was accompanied by another nigga that did not have the supporting gear on.

"Say ma cozz…. My big bro Body told me to check on his Lil caramel sit-u-ation. That nigga told me you was gonna have that Face Nation gear on your body. Its ya boy Money Bags but call me Money and this nigga right here is Des." Money said while doing some type of hand motions that

kind of resembling dance moves as he
introduces the nigga with him.

The two men looked nothing a like
Money was full of tattoos from his
face to his arms. Under all that ink
laid a handsome chocolate man. You
could tell he was young not only by
his energy level but also by his baby
face. On the other hand, Des looked
worn out and tired. It was also easy to
tell he used heavy drugs and was most

likely the same age as Money.

Something about him didn't sit right

with Dana, so she didn't even

acknowledge his presence.

"Nigga don't just run up on a

motherfucker like that I almost

painted the town red," Dana said

while turning in the direction of her

car.

"Ya boy Money here to walk you to your whip and protect the bag. Them jack boys be quick to try ta swipe."

"Trust me I can handle myself."

The short walk to her car was very entertaining. Money talked, joked, and dance the entire way there, stopping along the way fist bumping, shaking hands, and hugging people. It was clear he and his siblings were well known. Des did not say anything he just stayed close as he shift his site from the bag Dana carried to Money. Dana found it kind of odd, but she pushed those thoughts to the back of her head. From the walk home to the drive home she did not run into one obstacle.

Body had Dana meet him in the back

room at a washeteria. After typing the

four-digit code on the keypad, she

was let into a room with Body and

two other guys sitting at a round table.

One of the two guys she recognized; it

was Body's younger brother Money.

The other guy looked like a man of

little words, but he was very

handsome. He was dark-skinned with

short hair, but his features look as if God took his time carving him.

Money was busy passing bundles of bills through a money counter. Body was removing black wrapped packages out of bags of beads, and the mysterious man was weighing each package. Body picked his head up and looked in the direction of Dana.

"Wuzzam...Lil mama I see you can hang with the Gorillas out here in the

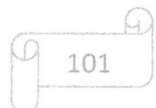

jungle." Body said while not even losing his stride on the task at hand.

Dana dropped her book bag of packages onto the table and said, "I would not consider such a country ass town a jungle."

Body laughed and turned to the mysterious guy at the table and said, "Look this my hitta and brother Bun that nigga got what you need."

Bun took a paper out of his black shirt pocket and handed it to Dana. Dana opened the paper and saw there was a Houston, Texas address written on the paper. Her heart raced, and her hands began to sweat; she was not good at hiding her emotions.

"The way you rubbing your tittie and got your mouth all twisted says your visit to these people ain't about to be a friendly one," Bun said while he rubbed his full beard.

"Chitty Chitty bang bang my coz…. aww yea ma coz aww yea she finesse right quick." Money said while he passed another bundle of cash through the counter.

"That's what the fuck you had me get my people to work on+, you one crazy bitch……but I like your ass." Body said while handing Dana the book bag along with a fat envelope

back without even attempting to

remove anything out of the bag.

"Look the slimy ass people I had

you'll search for hurt someone really

close to me and its time I pay them a

visit, but besides that what you hand

me this shit for," Dana said while

holding the bag out like it was

diseased.

"That shit needs to be delivered to Brownsville Texas, and since you going in that direction, you minus well do ya nigga that favor. My nigga Bun tagging with you because shit gets hectic around the drop."

"Here you niggas go thinking I can't handle myself."

"It's not that baby we southern men like to protect the women in our family."

"Whatever. When is all this shit supposed to go down?"

"You'll leave tomorrow at three a.m. sharp my people expect their product by lunch time."

"Bet," Dana said while walking out of the room. She was off to prepare for her home going party and introduce the Davis family to Alissa's new additions.

Dana woke up early that morning and packed her backpack with the goodies she bought the night before and a change of clothes. In went her newly purchase hunting knife, her .357 revolver, some duct tape, and some tie straps. She also placed a black dress paired with some red bottom pumps into the back pack. She placed her trusty Glock right next to her heart and slipped on some Fashion Nova

jeans over her black lace bra and
matching boy short set. She finished
her look up with a black V-neck shirt
along with some black and white
Vans.

She pulled her long Brown hair into a
high bun, and she was out the door.

She knew them jeans were hugging
her ass and thighs just right because
when she entered the garage it looked
as if Bun saw a ghost.

"Boo nigga can say I have my ass and titties back," Dana said while pressing the button on the wall for the garage door to open.

Bun looked at her and rolled his eyes while exiting the garage and going to the driver side of a rented 2017 black Toyota Camry. The two was off to take the almost nine-hour drive to Brownsville to make the delivery. While on the ride the two talked about

everything from relationships to

childhoods. Dana now knew that

Body, Money, and Bun had a younger

sister that was a lawyer and an older

brother that own a construction

company. Bun now knew that Dana

was abused and because of that abuse,

she did not remember most of her

childhood because she would offend

blackout.

Getting closer to the drop off location they went from paved road to a rocky road where Bun got out and entered a code into a lock on a cattle gate. When Bun re-entered the car, he urges Dana to remember how they left the gate.

"Look at that gate well and make sure you remember if it was left open are closed." Bun said while typing something into his phone and

continuing to drive the car down the
gravel and dusty road.

"What's the big deal about the gate,"
Dana said as she looked at Bun in a
confused manner.

"Just know if we don't be careful, we
won't make it home for Christmas."

"Damn it's like that"

"This city is damn near on the border of Mexico people will do anything to be in the states.

 Let's not forget we not exactly church people spreading the gospel either."

"Well say less my dude I'm ready for whatever," Dana said while rubbing her left tit.

"Damn what don't you have in there?"

"You"

"Don't get me started."

They both could see what looked like an abandoned house in the distance. Bun slowly rolled up to the house and parked the car around the back of the house. They both got out of the car

and went around to the rear and got a
black duffle bag out of the trunk.

"Look let me do all the talking just
stand there and look like the snack
you are." Bun said while putting the
bag strap over his shoulder and
walking in the direction of the door on
the house.

"Cool deal, I don't mind being the eye
candy in the room," Dana said while
walking close behind Bun.

"That you are my friend that you are."

"Ahhh Ahh Ah"

The two entered the building and was greeted by the faint smell of urine.

The roof was all busted, and the walls were covered with rust stains, and dirt. They walked until they reached a dim lit room where a man laid on a nasty as mattress watching a big booty television. Next to him rested his Draco with extra clips. Bun

cleared his throat, and the man stood

up.

The whole transaction went quickly

and smoothly. Bun and Dana got back

in the car and headed back toward the

gate. When they approach the

entrance, they both notice that the

gate was now close when they clearly

both knew Bun left it wide open. As

the car came close to the gate, there

was movement from the nearby tree
line. Dana did not hesitate to reach
into her bra and pull out her best
friend. People with ski and clown
mask emerged. Before the two knew
it, the car was surrounded by the mask
men.

The men pulled the door open on
Dana's side and yanked her out of the
car. They pulled on her so hard and
fast that she fell out of the car on to

her face. Bun didn't even let the mask

men get a chance to touch him; he

removed himself from the car. Dana

was boiling, and all she could see was

red. She flipped over, like some type

of cartoon character, with her gun aim

and ready to shoot. Dana pulled the

trigger and shot one masked man in

the head and the other straight in the

chest.

The noise of the shots made the other two masked men take their eyes off Bun and look to see if their fellow carjackers were alright. As soon as they forgot their mission Bun found his. He delivered a TKO blow to the masked man on his right jawline and grabbed the neck of the other guy and slit his throat with his pocket knife. The guy instantly grabbed for his neck as blood poured out wildly.

Dana got up off the ground and went over to Bun's side. She looked at his wet work and shook her head. "Not bad, but with that dull ass knife, you got that nigga might survive," Dana said as she aimed the gun she still held in her hand at the leaking man. POW! POW! She shot that nigga twice in the chest. He immediately stops moving. She was on a roll she saw the other nigga move, so she shot his ass too. POW! POW! POW! Two to the body and one to the head.

Bun just stood there looking at Dana admiring her skills and her crazy side. He was a hit man, but he never saw a woman slimy like this. Curiosity grows inside him, so Bun bent down to unmask the man with the slit throat.

He uncovered the man's face, and to his surprise, he knew exactly who the person was.

"MAN! I know this Lil crackhead as nigga, Des." Bun said as he kicked that nigga head like he was trying for a field goal.

"I knew something wouldn't right with that nigga when Money introduced his ass at the parade the other day," Dana said while folding her arms beneath her breast.

"My Lil bro ain't the best judge of character."

"Well, Lucifer will be the judge of that nigga now," Dana said while walking to the other side of the car like she just didn't help take the life of four men. She hopped in the car and sat there looking at Bun look at the bodies. Dana beeps the horn, so he could get moving because she was ready to get to the real action.

After passing the rented car through a
car wash and stopping at a truck stop
to freshen up and change clothes the
two were off to Houston. The sun was
slowly setting as Bun maneuvered the

Camry through traffic on the busy Texas highway.

He would catch himself sneaking peaks at Dana because she changed out of her jeans, t-shirt, and shoes into a tight body-hugging black dress with black, red bottom pumps. Her hips were so succulent in that dress. She had now released her brown curly hair from the updo, and it draped her shoulders making her facial features

pop. She was applying blush and red
lipstick as they cruise the highway.
She finished her look with three
sprays of Coco Chanel Mademoiselle
perfume.

"Damn who you are going meet like
that one of your old situations." Bun
said while he switched lanes.
"Na, fam just gotta look the part,"
Dana said while saving her cosmetics
in her book bag.

"Well you look nice, and you smell good enough to eat."

"Look don't start because I usually don't pass on the opportunity to get sucked on like an oxtail bone."

Bun laughed. Dana was still looking in the small visor mirror when she acknowledges Alissa about her part in tonight's activities. "I need you to play that Lil innocent school girl roll so we can get inside the house. If that

nigga Harold there he not gonna resist
all this, but if it's just that bitch Gwinn
don't worry, I got her." Dana said.

"Who the fuck are you talking to
Dana?" Bun said with a confused look
on his face.

"I'm not talking to you. I'm talking to
my bestie, my sister, Alissa."

"Woman, we the only people, in here
so who the fuck is ALISSA?"

"Yes, Alissa is always here; we share the same space," Dana said while pointing to her chest.

"So, you certifiable Crazy?"

"Na, Nigga Alissa is the one that suffered all the abuse as a child. Somehow some way through all of that anguish I was created. I like to think I am her protector."

"Oh, so you like an alter ego."

"Na, nigga I'm my own person some of the things I do Alissa won't even remember."

"So, like a split personality."

"Yea."

"Great now he gonna think we crazy as fuck. Good job Dana you the true MVP." Alissa said.

"Na, He cool people. I think he understands our situation, right."

Dana said while looking in the direction of Bun.

Bun didn't really understand what was going on, but he knew that Dana or Alissa had been through a lot. He wanted to let whoever he was talking to know he had they back, besides

whoever murdered those men had his back one hundred percent. Bun just nodded his head and exit off the highway in the direction of the Davis address.

"So where does the Davis family fit into all of this?" Bun said as he turned a corner. He glanced at Dana and notice her head was down with no motion coming from the rest of her body. He called out to her several times, with no answer.

Dana head slowly began to rise. As she picked up her head, she looked out the car window. "Mr. and Mrs.

Davis did terrible things to me. At

first, everything was good until it

wasn't anymore. I was basically their

slave. Mr. Davis wanted sex, but Mrs.

Davis was the devil herself. She

would burn cigarettes on me, sit on

my face, beat me with switches 2 by 4

pieces of woods, brass knuckles and

all kinds of stuff. The worst part about

it all was she use to sell my young

pussy and sit there and watch as I was raped by multiple men as I cried"

Bun could feel the pain in the young lady's voice. It was like her presence was pure and sweet, totally different from Dana's aura. He instantly understood why she developed Dana; she won't have survived if she had to endure it all alone.

"Damn, that's some sick shit. Well, let's slide on your foster parents with they bitch ass and repay their unwanted actions with some pain and pleasure. You ready shorty?" Bun said turning the car down the street that the Davis reside.

The subdivision was fully developed now from when Alissa was younger. The Davis's house was one out of three on the whole street. Now the street was filled with identical houses that ranged from level to two stories.

The only way she could tell they were
to the right home was the ugly ass
Winnebago that sat in the

driveway. That's where she was sold
at just the thought along sent chills
down her back.

She thought to herself that she
wouldn't be able to go through with
the plan, but Dana helps push that to
the back of her head. Bun could see
the anxiety building in Alissa so he

grabbed her hand and assured her he
wouldn't be far away. Bun stopped in
the middle of the street and went
around back of the car. He returned a
few minutes later with the license
plate. He then removed a white paper
and put it over the VIN that was in the
lower half of the driver side of the
windshield. He parked the car at an
abandoned house two houses down
from the Davis house.

Alissa was nervous, but she got out of the car and walked to the house with the raggedy yard, no lights on the outside, and the broke down Winnebago in the driveway. She noticed there were no lights on in the house as she got closer but could hear noise from the television. Harold always loves to have the television at the maximum sound. As she got closer to the door Bun tapped her on the shoulder and signal that he would

be waiting right on the side of the

house.

Alissa walked up to the door the

palms of her hands were sweating,

and she became weak in the knees.

She held onto the frame of the door to

catch her balance and calm down.

After a few seconds, Alissa built the

courage to knock on the door. She

tapped on the door very softy at first

then a little harder. Alissa waited a

few minutes before attempting to

knock again. As she raised her hand

to knock again, she saw the doorknob

move. The door creeps open.

Harold opened the door and looked

Alissa from head to toe taking in

every curve in her

form-fitting dress. "I don't know what

you selling but put me down for a

dozen," Harold said while holding

onto the outside of the

doorknob.

Alissa shifted her weight to one hip

and moved her hair to the back of her

shoulders. "I'm not selling anything

silly a girl can't come back to visit her

folks," Alissa said while leaning in

and touching Harold on the shoulders.

Harold began to stare into Alissa's eyes. It was no way he could forget her beautiful green eyes. "Alissa." He said while moving to the side to welcome her into their home. He took no time violating her when he tapped her on the ass as she walked into their house. The house had a faint smell of beer and cigarettes. They still had the oversized black sectional sofa and the

same white tile floor. The site of the
house made Alissa gag.

"Who's that at the door, Harold?"
Gwinn said from a distance.

"It's Alissa baby you remember
Alissa. Come outside and see her; she
all grown up now." Harold said while
grabbing a hand full of Alissa's ass.

Alissa did not move as she felt Harold
move so close to her that she could

feel his breath on her neck. Alissa heard footsteps approached them, she was sure it was Gwinn entering the room. She was right, the site of Gwinn along made Alissa light headed and dizzy. Gwinn looked Alissa up and down.

"Hmmm…What the fuck you doing here?" said Gwinn as she strolled slowly to meet Harold and Alissa who was still standing by the door.

"I huh just wanted to visit you'll," Alissa said as she wiped her sweaty palms on to the sides of her dress.

By this time Gwinn was standing in front of Alissa and Harold was in the back the three made a sandwich.

"You not just here to look bitch you here to get fucked you raggedy slut," Gwinn said while reaching up and grabbing Alissa's left breast. Harold got closer to Alissa and rubbed his dick onto Alissa's ass while he whispered, "This is what you want."

"Well bitch we don't fuck old bitches such as yourself we need young tender meat, so you need to get the fuck before our new meat see you here," Gwinn said while pushing Dana into Harold. "Get this thirsty bitch out of here before I fulfill my promise to her from many years ago."

Anger ate at Alissa as Dana slowly emerged and Alissa went to her safe place. It was time for these dirty old people to pay for all the things they put Alissa through.

Dana felt Harold's hands roughly grab her and push her to the door. Dana moved quickly as she grabbed the hunter's knife out of a garter holster. Dana turned swiftly and sliced Harold's ugly black face wide open.

Harold grabbed for Dana, and as he reached out, she came down with the knife with so much force that she sliced off all his fingers. He screamed in pain.

"I bet you won't put them midnight ass hands on another soul you sick ass pervert," Dana said as she began to kick Harold in his stomach. She notices that Gwinn was charging toward her, so she pulled out her

Glock out of its usual hiding spot, she pointed at Gwinn.

"Sit cho sick ass down and watch. I thought you like to watch people get tortured," Dana said as she bent down and stabbed Harold in the side of his neck.

Harold grabbed for his neck, and he opened his mouth wide. Dana slid the gun back into her bra and grabbed Harold's dick with one hand and slice that shit off with her other hand, pants

and all. She took the dismembered

body part and placed it into his

opened mouth and muffled his

screams. Dana could see from her

peripheral vision the glow of a cell

phone coming from the direction of

Gwinn. She pulled out her gun and

shot Gwinn in the left shoulder.

Gwinn dropped the phone and

screamed in pain. Dana moved toward

the phone.

"Shut up trick before I shoot, you

again," Dana said while she picked up

the phone off the floor to see the

numbers 91 dialed on the screen.

Dana became enraged by the thought

of this bitch wanting to call for help.

She went up to Gwinn and pistol-

whipped her so hard that she felt her

jaw shatter and teeth flew from her mouth.

"You gets nothing freak, but this punishment from these paws bitch," Dana said as she raised her hands up to Gwinn.

Harold started to move toward the door, so Dana ended him with two shots POW! One to the chest. POW! One straight to his black ass.

"Lay your nasty ass down old lady.

We about to have some fun bitch"

Dana told Gwinn as she turns and

headed toward the kitchen. She

noticed that there was a pot of water

on the stove and decided that's all she

needed to torture Gwinn.

She walked over to Gwinn looked

down at her and notice she was passed

out. Dana took the butt of her gun and

tapped on Gwinn's pale white

forehead. "Ahhh…you thirsty because you look thirsty old bitch," Dana said while holding the pot in one hand and her gun in the other. Gwinn shook her head wildly.

"Well,

You look thirsty to me, so I'm helping you out," Dana said as she took the pot and poured the boiling hot water over Gwinn starting at her head working down to her feet.

Alissa mentions to Dana she was doing too much and that she had been in the house a while and Bun was waiting for her outside.

"Lucky for you bitch I have other shit to do so I will give you the option to call for help one more time before I shot your brains out," Dana said while she put the pot down and held the phone out. Right before Gwinn grabbed for it, Dana forced Gwinn's legs open and shoved the phone up Gwinn's pussy.

"Let's see how a grown woman's pussy calls for help," Dana said while cocking her gun, looking Gwinn straight in the eyes and pulling the trigger. "See you in hell bitch."

Before leaving the house, Dana placed the pot back on the stove, pushed Harold's body closer to the door, and put Gwinn's body in her

bed. She found some lighter fluid in the garage and poured it next to the stove and on the murder locations. She picked up a book of matches off the table next to the sectional lit some of them and throw them next to the stove than lit the rest and throw them on the sofa where Gwinn was killed.

Dana walked out of the house and toward the rented car like a runway model as Bun tagged carefully

behind. The house started smoking in the background, Bun looked back to see a small flame growing inside of the home that Dana just left.

"Damn, Dana I could have helped you clean that shit up." Bun said while catching up to Dana.

"Nobody gonna cares about two pedophiles burning to death in a house fire," Dana said without even breaking a stride.

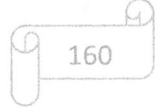

She reached the car and hopped into the driver seat. Bun opened the passenger side door and entered the vehicle. Before they exit the neighborhood, Bun removed his phone from his pocket found Body's contact and started a new message. "We found our new hitta. This bitch Dana Dangerous."

I'M A
BAD
GIRL

Don't Mess with ME!